Written by Brian Miles,
Illustrations by Ken McKie.

Published by
Grandreams Limited,
Jadwin House, 205/211 Kentish Town Road, London NW5 2JU.

Printed in Czechoslovakia.

ISBN 0 86227 898 8

KM41

Teddy Tales in this book

TEDDY and The Old Grange Mystery

The bears were in the chummery,
Talking of this and that.
Suddenly on the door,
There was a loud rat-a-tat-tat!

Teddy jumped up to open the door,
While the startled bears looked on.
But whoever it was at the door,
Now had most certainly gone!

On the ground however,
Teddy spotted a printed card.
He bent down to pick it up,
The others looked at it hard.

"It's an invitation," said Teddy,
Wearing a puzzled frown.
In eager anticipation,
The other bears sat down.

"Teddy, Jimbo, Bessy and Belle,
are invited to the Old Grange tonight.
Your esteemed presence is requested,
by your host who will be out of sight."

"The Old Grange is empty,"
said Bessy trying hard to smile.
"No-one has been living there,
for a very very long while."
"It sounds like a joke," said Jimbo, eating a bun.
"I vote that we should go, we're bound to have
some fun!"
FIZZ

At midnight's hour,
The village clock struck four.
"That's odd," said Teddy,
"there should be eight more."

With torches flashing,
The intrepid four,
Opened the gates,
And walked up to the door.

Teddy banged the knocker,
And bells started to ring!
"Hello!" he called,
And a statue began to sing!

The door creaked open,
Gingerly they stepped inside.
Then the door slammed shut,
And they all began to hide!

Bessy dived into a chest,
And Belle behind some armchairs.
Jimbo leaped inside a clock,
Which began to walk upstairs!

Teddy astride a moose's head,
Called out, "Is anyone there?"
"Of course there is," said a ghostly voice,
"we're all upstairs, down here!"

Suddenly a white sheet jumped up, and made a moaning sound.

Teddy fell off the moose's head and landed on the ground!

There were shouts and hoots of laughter,
And lights flashed off and on.
Belle was leaning against a bookcase,

Suddenly she was gone.

Sheets were bobbing up and down,
In the lofty baronial hall.
A smiling knight with his head under his arm,
Leaned against the wall.

Jimbo fell out of the Grandfather clock,
Somersaulting down the stairs.
He landed in an untidy heap,
On top of the other two bears.

When Teddy opened a cupboard door,
A grinning skeleton dropped his jaw.
Jimbo touched a panel and disappeared,
While from the bookcase Belle reappeared.

Down in the cellar an organ was playing.
Said Bessy, "That's enough, I'm not staying!"
Jimbo said, "Don't be hasty, leaving so soon.
Anyway I like it, they're playing our tune."

A dinner gong sounded,
By the dining room door.
So they all rushed in,
To find lovely food galore!

There were tarts and jellies, flans and apple pies.
The bewildered bears, could hardly believe their eyes.

The bears tucked in, and had a lovely time.
Then the big Grandfather clock began to chime.

"Goodness," said Teddy, "we've been here all night."
He opened the curtains, to sunshine bright.

The bears were sorry to leave the Grange,
Having had lots of fun.
Grateful to their invisible host,
And for his splendid pun.

The bears closed the garden gates,
In grateful appreciation.
And hoped it would not be long,
Before the next invitation.

TEDDY
Goes On Stage

Meandering through the forest
in the merry month of May,
Teddy heard a loud voice command,
"It's time to start the play."
Beckoning to the other bears
and then walking towards the sound,
They were very surprised to see
lots of bears seated all around.

"Sshh! Sit down!" said a nice young bear,
"the play's just about to start.
This scene is extremely funny,
and she's perfect for the part."

The play indeed was very funny,
And they quickly began to laugh.
Especially when a bear came on,
And tripped over his bright red scarf!

The bears all laughed and clapped aloud,
As the play came to an end.
The director said, "That was good!
But who's our little friend?"

Teddy stood up and introduced himself,
And then, Jimbo, Bessy and Belle.
"I'm pleased to meet you," the director said,
" and to see you looking so well."

The director bear wore a monocle,
And a green polka dot bow tie.
He said, "I'm glad you stayed to watch our play."
Said Teddy, "We were just passing by."

"We are a band of strolling players,
ever travelling from town to town.
We are a most happy company,
I'm Sir Humphrey Eiderdown."

"Tomorrow we start rehearsals,
for a really big new show.
If you can play an instrument,
I'll be very glad to know."

“I can play drums,” said Teddy,
“and Jimbo plays saxophone.
Bessy plays the double bass,
and Belle the slide trombone.”

"That's wonderful!" Sir Humphrey cried,
"we'll give a gala show.
We'll get all the bears for miles around,
I'm sure they'll come, you know."

"Now listen to me everybody,
we all know what has to be done.
Scenery to paint and costumes to make,
It will be a lot of good fun!"

The clearing then became noisy,
Bears hammered, painted and sawed.
All the bears were very busy,
There was no chance to be bored.

"You can take charge of ticket sales,"
Sir Humphrey said to Teddy.
"Why don't you take the bus on a tour,
when can you be ready?"
"We'll leave first thing in the morning,"
Teddy was delighted to say.
"From a mobile ticket office,
we can sell tickets all the way."

And so off went the bears the next morning,
At dawn's early light.
Sir Humphrey Eiderdown's Theatre Bus,
Made a splendid sight.

The bears travelled from village to village,
And then from town to town.
Selling tickets from the box office bus,
To all the bears around.

Then back to the theatre in the wood,
Having sold every seat.
Sir Humphrey pleased with their excellent work,
Gave them all a lovely treat!
There were scrumptious cakes and jellies,
And jugs of iced lemonade.
The bears tucked in and filled their tums,
Then went to sleep in the shade.

Now was the night of the concert,
And the audience had grown large.
At last Sir Humphrey came on stage,
And said, "Good evening, I'm in charge!"

The audience laughed
and the show began,
A magician appeared
and waved a fan.

There was a Juggler
on a tightrope,

And then at last came the Grand Finale,
With Teddy and the Big Bear Band.

A trick cyclist
on his bike.

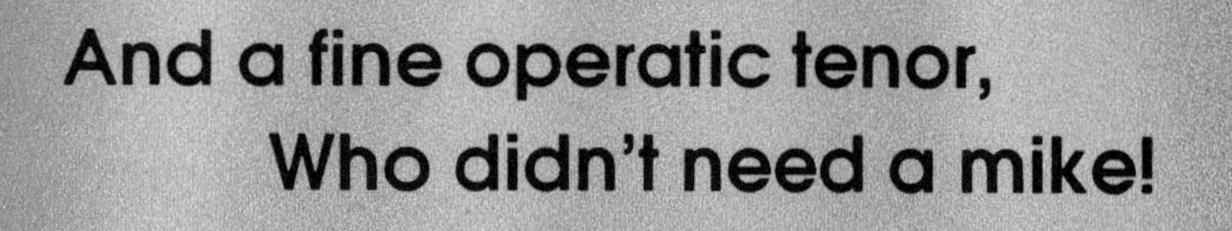

And a fine operatic tenor,
Who didn't need a mike!

Their playing of 'At The Woodchopper's Ball',
Could be heard all over the land.

The audience clapped and whistled,
And the woods echoed to their cheers.
And everyone was agreed,
It was the biggest show in years.
Sir Humphrey shook hands with Teddy,
And said, "I am in your debt.
Tonight's success is owed to you,
and that I will never forget."

Teddy and the bears wished Sir Humphrey
And the Company, "Goodbye!"
And hoped to see them again one day
When they were passing by.

TEDDY
and
The Teddy Bear Jamboree

The bears were in their little hut,
Which they called `the chummery'.
Bessy had just boiled a kettle,
For a pot of Earl Grey tea.

"I've been thinking," said Teddy Bear,
"how very nice it would be,
if we could stage a grand event,
like a Teddy Bear Jamboree."

"We'll tell the woodland birds," said Teddy,
"to spread the word far and wide.
And every bear will be invited,
throughout the whole countryside."

"But just wait a moment," Jimbo said,
"we shall have to tell the Mayor.
The bears of the village must be asked,
after all that's only fair."

"Then let's not waste time," cried Teddy,
"there's not a moment to be lost.
We'll ask the Mayor to approve our plan,
and invite him to be the host."

"Splendid idea!" the Mayor exclaimed,
When he heard of Teddy Bear's plan.
"This will bring all bears together,
like a gathering of the clan."

So the bears began to prepare,
For the exciting day ahead,
As they put up flags and bunting,
Of blue and white, yellow and red.

They painted the village hall,
And erected a huge marquee.
Then at last they were ready,
For the Teddy Bear Jamboree.

As dawn broke over the village,
A wondrous sight could be seen.
Hundreds of bears from all around,
Gathered on the village green.

They had come in buses and coaches,
Motor cars and bikes as well.
And Town Crier Bear walked through the throng,
Happily ringing his bell.
"Oyez! Oyez! you Teddy Bears,"
he cried out so merrily.
"You are welcome one and all,
to the Teddy Bear Jamboree."

There were games and competitions,
For the biggest this and that.
And Bessy won a silver cup,
For the most outrageous hat!

Mr. Bruin Bear's marrow,
Was the biggest ever seen.
And Jock McBear from Scotland,
Had the longest runner bean!

The dancing bears from Penge,
Stepped daintily around the floor.
And eight big bears from Dorchester,
Then won the Tug-o-War!

The flower arrangement contest,
Was won by Miss Pansy Bear.
Who also won `The Best Gurney',
Which she'd entered for a dare.

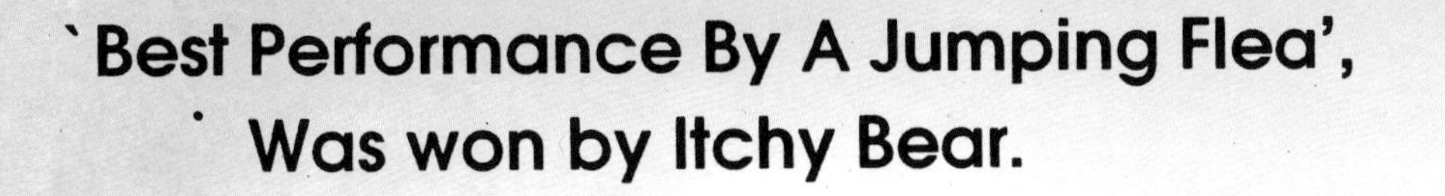

`Best Performance By A Jumping Flea',
Was won by Itchy Bear.

Who then said, "It was nothing really,
I've plenty more so there!"

There was dancing around the maypole,
And lots of gadding about.
For when Teddy Bears have a good time,
They all love to laugh and shout.

The top award for the loveliest rose,
Was won by Mr. Smelly Bear.
Who also won the best perfume award,
For an aroma described as rare!

The prize for the best pot of jam,
Was an extremely sticky choice.
Especially when the village Mayor,
Unfortunately lost his voice!

Captain Boggles and his daring bears,
Put on a flying display.
Whilst the band of the Grenadier Bears,
Began playing `Blaze Away'.

Free-fall parachute bears,
Were dropping all around,
Just as the Mayor announced,
His voice had just been found!

The Jamboree was a huge success,
Thanks to Teddy's great idea.
"Thank you all for coming," said the Mayor.
"Let's do it again next year."

TEDDY
and
The Secret Garden

Deep in the heart of the forest,
Beneath the tall greenwood trees,
The bears were cooking their supper,
Fanned by a cool summer breeze.

"This expedition," said Jimbo,
"was a jolly good idea.
And when we have put this tent up,
we'll have some cold ginger beer."

Bessy and Belle were cooking,
Something tasty in the pan.
"When we have had our supper,
we'll sit and study the plan."

When they had finished eating,
Teddy lit the lamp.
Then the bears sat on the ground,
In their woodland camp.

"Our path tomorrow," said Teddy,
tapping the map with a stick,
"will lead us to parts unexplored,
where the trees are very thick."

So the bears settled down for the night,
Beneath a starlit sky.
Watched from a tree by old wise grey owl,
With his unblinking eye.

They awoke with a start the next morning,
To a cacophony of sound.
The birds were whistling, the bees were buzzing,
The woods were alive all around.

They folded their tent and packed their kit,
Then bathed beneath a waterfall.
With packs on their backs they started out,
Down a path flanked by trees so tall.

At first, the path they followed
was very broad and clear,

But as the day wore on,
it began to disappear.

Teddy with puzzled expression
looked at the map again,

"We're lost," he suddenly cried,
and then it started to rain.

They ran for shelter by a high stone wall,
But then were most startled to hear a call:
"I say you young bears, be of good cheer.
Find the steps in the wall, and come over here."

The bears scrambled over,
To see who was there,
And were surprised to see,
A charming old bear.

"I'm a hermit bear, I live here all alone,
this huge walled garden is my secret forest home.
But I like to see some visitors now and then,
please join me for tea in my cosy little den."

The sun came out again,
as they walked into the den.
Hermit made a pot of tea,
and said his name was Ben.
"I've lived here all alone," said he,
"since I was a little cub.
I don't see many others bears,"
and he gave his eyes a rub.

"Don't cry," said Teddy, "we'll be your friends,
and we'll come to see you at weekends."
"Oh, that would be lovely," Ben declared,
"let's have some tea, it's all prepared.
There's bread and scones, and honey from my bees,
and a cake full of plums from my own trees."

The hungry bears enjoyed
A most delightfully scrumptious tea.
Then Ben said, "I'll show you my garden,
it's lovely as you'll see."
He gave them each a large basket,
And smiling said, "Follow me.
First we'll go to the orchard,
and you can pick from every tree."

They picked apples, plums and pears,
Shaped just like a bell.
Then cherries and greengages,
And damsons as well.

Then to the vegetable garden,
So tidy and neat,
To pick carrots, peas and lettuces,
And parsnips so sweet!

There were potatoes,
Cauliflowers and cabbages galore.
But at last their baskets were full,
And could not take anymore.

"This is most kind of you,"
Teddy said to Ben,
"but look at the time,
it's almost half past ten."
Said Ben, "Please do not worry, be my guests tonight.
You can leave in the morning, by dawn's early light."

The bears were glad to stay,
With good and kindly Ben.
He said, "There's plenty of room,
in my cosy den."

"Let's have an old-time music evening,"
Ben said with a smile.
"I will play the piano,
in my own particular style."

So they gathered around the piano,
And sang along with Ben.
And they all joined in the chorus,
When Bessy sang, `We'll Meet Again'.

As the bears left in the morning,
They promised Ben, "We'll see you soon."
And as they walked through the forest,
They heard a familiar tune.
It was Ben at his grand piano,
Playing that old song again.
He was very happy now,
And it was all because of the rain.